ARE YOU COMFORTABLY?

Stories for Retelling

by

ALYN HASKEY

MOORLEY'S Print & Publishing

llustrated by Dean Brookes.

ISBN 0 86071 352 0

MOORLEY'S Print & Publishing
23 Park Rd., Ilkeston, Derbys DE7 5DA
Tel/Fax: (0115) 932 0643

FOREWORD

The radio was switched on. It was nearly time, then I would hear the words that were the highlight of my day, "Are you sitting comfortably? Then I'll begin."

As a child I loved to hear stories. There is always great excitement imagining the action especially if the story teller was skilful. In turn I would be gripped, amused, maybe even frightened, all this without even the hint of a TV screen or a video.

Jesus was famous for his stories, crowds would gather round him to hear him talk about lost sheep, parties or good neighbours. He took everyday subjects and through them proclaimed the gospel. Here are a collection of stories that seek to do the same. I still enjoy stories, and I hope you do too.

THE KITE

There was a boy called David who loved to fly kites. First of all he would build them. Then he would attach the string and then, when the weather was just windy enough, he would take his kite to the biggest open space he could find, and let his kite fly in the air.

One day David got up very early, took his kite and went out. It was just the right weather he thought, so gradually he let the kite go higher and higher and higher. But as the day went on the wind began to get stronger and David found it more difficult to control the kite. He had to pull really hard. And the wind got stronger and stronger until suddenly the kite was blown right into a tree and it got stuck. What's more, it was the biggest tree you have ever seen.

David pulled on the kite but it wouldn't come, he tried to shake the tree but still the kite wouldn't move. What could he do? There was nobody around and in any case the tree was far too high to climb. He decided that the wind wasn't a very good friend. He began to wish that there was no such thing as the wind.

Then he remembered that the person who made the wind was also the person who helped people. He wondered if that person could release the kite. But then he thought how do you ask him? He'd been told you could talk to him anywhere so he thought he'd try it, "Hey you, who made the wind, could you help me get my kite back?" He waited. At first nothing happened, but then the wind changed direction, and the kite flew free. David was excited. "Thankyou", he shouted, "I want to be your friend." So David got his kite back and that day he decided he'd find out more about the person who made the wind.

AN IMPORTANT JOB

Keith was fed up, and the reason he was fed up was because in the church everybody had important jobs to do but all he did was go to Sunday School. He didn't think that was a job at all, all the other jobs were much more important.

One day he decided he wanted to be a missionary, they had exciting jobs - they went overseas to tell the Good News. But then he realised he couldn't be a missionary because he didn't like hot weather and he didn't like cold weather either, and what's more he was a bit young.

Another day he decided he was going to be a Vicar, that was an important job - all those people to look after. But then he was also a bit young for that, and besides you have to do a lot of studying before you could become a Vicar. Perhaps he could be a Church Warden - but you have to be quite old and dress in suits for that. Oh dear he thought, there just isn't a job that I can do.

The Vicar noticed that Keith was unhappy. Keith said, "I just can't find an important job." Then the Vicar said a strange thing (Vicars do that sometimes), "You are very good at Sunday School aren't you? You get very high marks and do very good work." "But that's not an important job", said Keith. The Vicar showed him that it was important. First - because he was learning about Jesus and the Bible and that would be important as he grew up. And secondly - because people read what Keith wrote and looked at his pictures so they too could learn about Jesus. So Keith realised that no matter how small the job was, it was still important.

THE MOVE

Davy was ten years old. He had always lived in the town and he enjoyed it, especially the school around the corner. His favourite subject was history, but he liked the other subjects as well. He had lots of friends and they played exciting games.

One day, Davy got some bad news. His dad had got a new job, so they had to move. Davy was not happy at all. He didn't want to leave his friends and his school.....and the ice cream shop on the corner. He thought about running away, but he had always been told that that wasn't a good thing to do. There was no choice. This made him even more sad. What made it worse was that he didn't even know anything about the place they were going to!

His dad said to him, "Cheer up, David! I know you don't want to move, but I'll make you a promise. I'm sure you'll make lots of new friends and that you'll be happy." Davy wasn't so sure, but he loved dad and so he waited to see what would happen.

The day for the great journey came. It was quite a long one. By car, then train, and even by aeroplane. Finally, they arrived at their new home. It didn't look very good, but dad said that some friends were going to help to decorate it and make it look good. But do you know, an amazing thing happened! There were lots of new friends for Davy to play with, just as dad had promised, and he was very happy in his new home.

WAITING FOR A TRAIN

Robby was excited. This was the day he had been waiting for for a long time. He was going on holiday to the seaside, but what made it more exciting was that he was going by train. He loved to travel on trains and this was to be a very long journey and would involve changing trains.

He arrived at the station and picked up his ticket. Then, as he got to the platform, he took out the instructions that he'd been given. The piece of paper said that he should wait for the 10.30 train. But that was over half an hour to wait and, at that moment, he heard the announcer say that the train that was standing at the platform was going to the same place. Robby couldn't understand why he shouldn't catch this first train as it would leave in five minutes. Surely it would get him there much quicker.

Now Robby was a sensible boy, so instead of just jumping on the train, he thought he had better ask somebody. He found a porter and asked him why he shouldn't catch the first train. The porter explained to him why it wouldn't be a good idea. He said, "This train leaves earlier, but it gets there later." "I see", said Robby. "If I took this train, I would miss my connection and my friends and that would spoil my day, so I'd better wait here and obey the instructions and then everything will work out." And that's exactly what happened, it did all work.

THE HAPPY MAN

Once, there was a town where all the children were sad. They never played games and never laughed. Not because they didn't want to, but because their king said they mustn't.

The king was even more unhappy than the children. He didn't like games, didn't like jokes and, most of all, he didn't like people laughing at all.

Now one day, when the town was quiet as usual, suddenly, there was a strange noise. Everybody stopped. The noise grew louder and louder and louder until, finally, they could see what it was. There was a stranger and he was.....laughing! The children were all amazed. They never had seen anyone laugh. "Hello", said the stranger, "I'm the happy man, I've come to make everybody laugh. Will you come and join me, and play some games?"

At first they weren't too sure, but he laughed so much that they began to laugh. First a snigger which they tried to stop quickly; but soon they couldn't hold it any longer. They all burst out laughing. They had a wonderful time, playing all sorts of games.

Suddenly there was a shout, "Here comes the king!" Everything went quiet. All the children were frightened. The king looked very cross. "What is all this noise?", he shouted. "Who has been laughing? You know it isn't allowed. Who is it? Come on, tell me." Now one little boy was so frightened by the king that he said, "It was him." and pointed to the stranger. The king looked at the Happy Man, "So you're the cause of the trouble then? Well you won't laugh again!" He called his soldiers over, "Take him to the deepest dungeon in the castle and lock him in, and nobody will hear him again." So they did that, they took him to the deepest, to the darkest dungeon and locked the door and left him there. The children were even sadder than before.

But that's not the end of the story. Three days later, when the castle was all quiet, and the king was sitting on his throne, he heard a strange noise. It sounded like laughter and it grew louder, and louder, and louder, and the building began to shake. "Stop it!" the king shouted, "stop it, stop it, stop it!" But, no matter how much he shouted, the laughter kept on. And at that time, all the doors of the dungeons flew open and all the people who had been kept locked up for laughing were set free and they all came to see the king. And who was leading them, but the Happy Man! When the king saw them, he ran and ran and I think he's still running today. From that day on, there was laughter instead of sadness and the children played lots of games and enjoyed themselves.

THE SHEPHERD

Once upon a time, there was a flock of sheep. They were pretty ordinary sheep and, yet, in one sense they were very fortunate because they were looked after by a very good shepherd. Day by day, he made sure that they had plenty of pasture to eat and water to drink. And every night, he made sure that they were safe inside the fold, and he himself would sleep across the door so that no one could get in.

Now, one day a little black sheep had run away. At first the shepherd did not know; but when he counted his sheep, he discovered that one was missing. So, immediately he set out: he climbed the rocks and walked down the valleys, searching high and low, until he found it, and when he saw it, he picked it up and put it on his shoulder and carried it home, back to safety.

On another occasion, a fierce wolf tried to get into the fold late at night, and the shepherd woke up and wrestled with the wolf. The wolf bit him two or three times very badly, but the shepherd continued to struggle until the wolf finally ran away and peace was restored.

Now, in the district at this time, were two ruthless and evil men who made their money by selling what wasn't theirs'. They were getting short of cash so they decided to do something about it. Seeing that the shepherd had such a good flock, they decided that they would try to steal some of his sheep. They did not really want to hurt the shepherd but they did not see how to get him out of the way. They crept up to the fold, but instead of entering through the door, they dug a hole through the side. But, as they crept in, the shepherd saw them and moved towards them. They tried to make him run away but he wouldn't go. He wanted to stay and protect his sheep so they set about him and eventually killed him. When they realized what they had done, they ran away.

The sheep were left without a shepherd. They were so lost and outside they could hear the wolves drawing near. Just then, a man appeared. He took the shepherd by the hand and raised him up. The sheep were so glad that he was alive. Now they felt safe and when the people heard about the shepherd, they sent their sheep to him, for they knew that he would take care of them.

SPECIAL AWARD

One day it was announced in school that there would be a special award for the best boy. Amongst the favourites were William and Timothy. Timothy could not understand why he was favourite but William immediately began to brag and boast. Of course he would win. Wasn't he the cleverest, bravest, most helpful? William sat down and began to think of all the good things he was. He was so proud and glad he was not like anybody else. How good he felt.

As Timothy sat down he tried to work out why his name was put down. He could not think of anything he was good at. No sports, no lessons, and as for helping people, he could not think of anything special he had done. In fact, compared to William, he was fairly average.

The day came for the presentation. There were many VIPs there and a tremendous sense of excitement. Who would win the prize? All the favourites sat together. At last the moment of truth came, the Headmaster stood up to announce the winner. William was already halfway to his feet to receive the award when he froze suddenly. The winner was Timothy. Timothy could not believe his ears. William did not feel at all well.

(Parable of the Pharisee and the Publican.)

THE FOREST RESCUE

The Smith family were on holiday. They were Mr. and Mrs. Smith, Kevin and John; an average family, except that Kevin was one of the most selfish children you could ever wish to meet. He was cheeky to Mr. Smith; he was rude to Mrs. Smith. And as for John, Kevin pushed him around. One day, when they were all watching television, Kevin wouldn't be quiet until he got his way which resulted in both Mr. and Mrs. Smith and Mr. Jones, the other guest, leaving the room. When John came in, Kevin decided he didn't want to watch television, and would not let John either. The day after, they all went out for a picnic and again Kevin showed his greed and selfishness, and as if that wasn't enough, he went off by himself, totally unaware of what the others wanted to do. But by the time it was getting dark, Kevin was lost and afraid - so were his parents. But John was in the Boy Scouts and he set out with his compass to find Kevin. When Kevin saw John he was so relieved, and yet so ashamed of all that he'd done, and when he got back to the car he promised never to be so blind or selfish again.

(Bartimaeus.)

THE SUBSTITUTE

One day, while the children were at school, and indeed should have been working, they decided instead to play games with a ball. Now Jimmy was not keen on this at all; he thought they should have been working. But Dennis who was never keen on school thought it a very good idea until the ball smashed the window which resulted in the headmaster visiting the class. He questioned the children one by one to try and find out who had thrown the ball through the window, but none of the children would own up. So he decided to keep all of them in until the culprit was found. At this point, Jimmy came forward and confessed that he had broken the window, much to everyone's surprise. He received the punishment and the children were dismissed. But Dennis was troubled for it was he who had thrown the ball through the window and couldn't understand why Jimmy had confessed. Jimmy replied that this was because he loved him.

(The Crucifixion.)

TODAY IS MY DAY

It was early in the morning when she dragged herself off her bed, as painful as usual, for twelve years she had been like this. She thought to herself, "Today could be different, it could be the beginning of a new life for He was coming and if she could get to him, well".

She hurried out, not waiting to eat, there was no time for that, there were already crowds of people around, then she saw Him. He was everything that she had heard. "Yes" she thought, "Today could be the day".

She pushed her way through the crowd, it wasn't easy. Many people were trying to reach Him, but as she drew near horror came upon her. "No!" she cried out, "He's been called away to heal someone's daughter". She became frantic, "You can't do this to me" she thought as she struggled towards Him. "Today is my day", her body was aching "He's my one hope, just to touch His cloak would be enough". She stretched out her hand, there it was; as she touched her pain stopped, but so had He and now He was asking who had touched Him. "Should I tell Him?" Again He asked. In a stumbling voice she said, "It was I, I touched you, I believed that you could heal me and it has happened". He looked at her and she felt a warm gentle love flow over her. He spoke softly yet firmly, "Your faith has made you whole - go in peace." As she walked home slowly she thought to herself, "Today is my day".

JACKIE'S BIG SURPRISE

Jackie was an average little girl except for one thing. She was always naughty. Of course, other kids are naughty at times, but at other times they're good, but Jackie was never good. To say she was eight years old, she had quite a reputation. This didn't make her very popular with anybody.

Jimmy was having a party. He was nine years old. The house was already full of friends who brought lots of lovely presents and there were sounds in every room of games being played. Suddenly there was a knock at the door. Jimmy's mother went to open the door. To her horror, there was Jackie. "Hallo" she said, "I've come to the party." Jimmy's mother said, "There's no way that you'll come to this party. Just go away until you can learn to behave." Jackie was sad.

Another time, all the children in Jackie's class were going on a picnic. It was a lovely day, lots of sunshine and there was great excitement, but when Jackie turned up, her teacher said, "I'm sorry but you can't come with us, you're far too naughty. You'll have to miss all the fun until you learn to behave." Jackie was even more sad. She began to see that being naughty wasn't much fun.

Jackie wanted to join the Brownies. She asked her mum to buy a uniform for her to wear and she went off to her first meeting, but when she got to the door, the Leader said, "I'm sorry Jackie, you can't possibly be a Brownie because they're good and you just can't behave". As Jackie walked away she began to cry.

As Jackie was walking in the park feeling very sad, she saw Mr. Niceman walking along. He was very happy today. Indeed he always seemed to be happy. He worked in the church and was very popular. He noticed Jackie and called for her. Jackie felt ashamed. She was far too naughty for Mr. Niceman to talk to her. She wanted to hide, but Mr. Niceman came to her. "Hello Jackie" he said, "I'm having a party and want you to come." Jackie was surprised, "Me" she said, "but I'm far too naughty, you can't possibly want me". "Yes I do" said Mr. Niceman. "But there are lots of people much better than me" said Jackie. "They're never naughty." "But I want you" said Mr. Niceman. "Will you come?" "Yes" said Jackie, and she went to the party and had a good time. And after that she wasn't naughty.

THE VISIT

This is the story of Jimmy. Jimmy was the worst boy in town; if there was a window broken anywhere you could be sure it was Jimmy; if there was a disturbance in the street you could be sure it was Jimmy. His Mum and Dad had nightmares about him, his teachers had given up and the only thing that was guaranteed to send people indoors in a hurry was Jimmy.

Now one day the town was in uproar, everybody was rushing around, there were ribbons flying across the streets and everyone was excited, and so they should be because a special person was coming to town. People were dressed in their best clothes because they all were hoping to talk to the guest. Now when Jimmy found out that the special guest was going to come right down his street he asked his Mum and Dad if he too could speak to this special guest, but they were horrified, and so were the neighbours. "Let Jimmy speak to our special guest, Jimmy, that troublemaker, the worst boy in town, not a chance. He must be kept out of the way to save embarrassment." So he was locked in a bedroom where he could see but hopefully could not cause any trouble.

Now Jimmy had other ideas, he knew that the special guest was coming down the street 'cos there was so much cheering but he couldn't see properly so he opened the window and he climbed up on the roof. He had a perfect view, but what he didn't realise was that the special guest also had a perfect view. He stopped walking, looked straight up at the roof and said, "Jimmy, come down here". Well, Jimmy was so surprised, he almost fell, but he managed to clamber down the drainpipe all the way to the ground. The neighbours were cross, why should a special person talk to the naughtiest boy in town. If ever there was any trouble in the town you could be sure it was Jimmy. Now when Jimmy stood in front of the special guest, the guest spoke again." Jimmy, I want you to do something for me." Well, Jimmy was excited but at the same time he felt ashamed. He said to himself, "He wants me to help him but I'm not good enough, I'm ever so naughty," and for the first time in his life he felt really sorry for what he'd done and his head hung down. "Jimmy" said the special guest, "would you help me?" "Yes I will" said Jimmy, "I will, but I've been very naughty and I'm so sorry and I want to help all the people I've upset." The special guest smiled, took Jimmy's hand and said, "Come with me".

The Son of Man came to seek the lost and to call Sinners to repentance.

THE WASHING

Once upon a time there was a little old lady called Mrs. Moffet, and one morning she had to do some washing. The reason why she had to do the washing was that she was going away that evening.

Mrs. Moffet put the washing into a bowl, filled it with water and began to wash. "Rub-a-dub, Rub-a-dub-dub" she sang to herself as she washed away. After some time she looked at the clock, 10.00 o'clock she thought, that's plenty of time, they must be clean now. So she pulled the clothes out of the water, but to her amazement they weren't clean. "Well" she thought, "I'll have to wash even harder".

She put fresh water in the bowl, she put the clothes in and began to wash again. Rub-a-dub-dub, Rub-a-dub-dub, she washed all the harder. After a while she thought to herself, "It must be clean now", so she took it out, looked at it and was utterly surprised, they were still dirty, she looked at the clock and it was dinner time.

After dinner she decided to use the washing machine. She filled it with water, put the clothes in and shut the door and pressed the button. Off it went - 'Splish-splash, round-and-round, splish-splash, round-and-round' - she pressed the button to stop it. Now she thought "They must be clean and I shall be able to go away". She took the clothes out but, oh dear, they still weren't clean.

She put the clothes back in, put the water in, shut the door, pressed the button. Off it went splish-splash, splish-splash, round-and-round, round-and-round - it went. After a while she pressed the button and stopped the machine. She took out the clothes, "Surely they were clean now". She looked, no, they still weren't clean. She looked at the clock and it was 4 o'clock, what could she do, another hour and she was going away.

Just then there was a knock at the door. She opened it and there was her friend Mrs. Thingummy. "Oh what can I do" she said, "I can't get my washing clean and I'm going away." Mrs.

Thingummy said, "Why don't you try washing powder?" "Washing powder. But surely you can wash clothes in just water?" "No, you need something to take away the stain". "All right, I'll give it a try".

So she put the water in, put the clothes in, added the powder and shut the door, and pressed the button, splish-splash, round-and-round, splish-splash, round-and-round it went. After a while she stopped the machine, she took out the clothes and looked at them and she was delighted, the clothes were as white as snow, so she was able to go away.

We are like dirty washing and we cannot be cleansed unless we come to Jesus and confess our sins. Only if we do this can we ever be made pure and white.

THE GREAT PARTY

Once upon a time there was a king and he decided to hold a great party in his palace. He invited all his subjects, amongst them were Mr. Allright-Jack and Mr. Always Loving.

Mr. Allright-Jack set out, as he was going along he met a man by the roadside and this man was shivering and cold and he said in a shaky voice, "Please Sir have you got a jacket to lend me".

Well! Mr. Allright-Jack stopped. "Give you my jacket, my best jacket! Not a chance, I'm on my way to see the king, I can't stop any longer" and off he went saying, "I'm allright, I'm o.k." Shortly after Mr. Always Loving came by and he too noticed the man by the roadside and the man said, "Please Sir could you lend me your jacket". Mr. Always Loving said, "I haven't got a very good one but here you are". So he gave him the jacket and he went on his way saying, "I'm happy".

Now Mr. Allright-Jack got near the palace and he noticed a man who was hungry and the man said, "Please Sir, have you got anything to eat". Mr. Allright-Jack said, "Give you something to eat. I have a big bar of chocolate but that's for me, not you." And he continued on his way saying, "I'm allright, I'm o.k." Now when Mr. Always Loving saw the man he felt sorry for him and even before the man could ask he said, "I've only a small biscuit, but here you are, you have it" and he went on his way saying, "I'm happy".

Now when they got to the palace the king welcomed everybody but he was especially pleased to see Mr. Always Loving. "Come in my friend, how welcome you are. I've heard you're so kind and always helpful. You come and sit by my side." Now after a while Mr. Allright-Jack noticed he'd been ignored so he called out "Your Majesty, you haven't forgotten me have you". Well, the king turned round and he looked very angry. "Just what makes you think that you're welcome here. You treated me cruelly; you wouldn't feed me or talk to me". Mr. Allright-Jack was amazed. "When did I see the king and not talk to him or feed him." The king said, "You didn't do it for anyone, so you didn't do it for me, go away".

And Jesus said:
"In as much as you didn't do it for one of these you didn't do it for me".

17

ALIVE!

Early on Sunday morning the two Mary's went to the garden. They just wanted to say goodbye to Jesus, their friend.

When they'd nearly reached the grave the whole place began to shake and the stone, which was heavy, rolled away. On it sat an angel dressed in white.

The two Mary's were frightened but not as much as the soldiers. They ran away. After a few seconds the angel spoke, "You've come to see Jesus, haven't you. Well, he's not here - look you can come and see for yourself! He is alive. Go and tell his friends that he will meet them in Galilee.

They ran away as quickly as they could. They were excited but frightened as well. Suddenly - there He was! Jesus - alive! They just didn't know what to think they were so overjoyed and excited. But Jesus reminded them that they had to tell his friends that they would see him later.

Meanwhile, the soldiers had gone back into the city and told the mourners what had happened and they decided that the best way to keep it quiet was to make up some stories. So they gave the soldiers a lot of money to say that Jesus' friends had come at night and taken him away.

Now Jesus' friends were all together and suddenly He was there! They couldn't believe it. Some rubbed their eyes because they weren't quite sure but they soon realised that it was Him. He told them that they had to go all over the world to tell people that Jesus was alive.

ANIMAL ACTS

CLARENCE THE CAT

Clarence was the biggest coward you could ever meet. Mice terrified him and when he saw dogs he panicked and one night, when he saw his own shadow he ran away.

Clarence didn't like being a coward and decided to seek help. The wisest person in the kingdom was Lord Lion. He knew the answers to thousands of questions. He was the one to see.

Having decided to see Lord Lion, Clarence was even scared of doing this but the alternative was to remain a coward so he went in. Lord Lion said to him.

"Go to the deepest, darkest part of the wood and wait until something happens."

And that was it. That was all he said.

Clarence didn't like dark, deep woods, especially at night, especially if it meant waiting there. He crept in, trembling, looking around, jumping at his own shadow, and waited, and waited, and waited. After a long time he began to wonder if it was worthwhile but he couldn't bear the thought of going back to Lord Lion having not obeyed him. So he waited, and waited, and waited. Then suddenly, there was a flash of lightning and a clap of thunder. Clarence shook. Then came another flash and clap and suddenly Clarence was no longer afraid. He didn't mind the darkness and the shadows, or the thunder. It meant that Lord Lion was right. He wasn't afraid any more. And he danced all the way home, shouting and singing.

MICKEY THE MONKEY

The news about Clarence spread rapidly. He was a very different cat now, cool, relaxed, but excited. He wanted to tell everybody what had happened to him and how Lord Lion had changed him.

One day he was walking along and he saw Mickey the monkey, he felt sorry for Mickey because unlike other monkeys he couldn't climb trees or swing about, he was very sad because he had a bad leg and couldn't play.

Clarence wondered if Lord Lion could help Mickey so he said to Mickey, "I think that if you believe in Lord Lion you could get better". Mickey wasn't too sure about this, after all, he had always had a bad leg, how could he change, just like that?" But Clarence was so insistent that Mickey said, "All right. I'll have a go". So he closed his eyes and said, "I believe in Lord Lion". And suddenly his leg began to feel better and in no time at all he was jumping, and in an even shorter time he was swinging in trees, shouting and singing. "Hey, look what happened to me! I'm better." All this noise brought the other animals rushing in. There was Redneck the snake, Ali the alligator, Eric the Eagle, Freddy the Fox and Tim the Tiger. They all wanted to hear what had happened.

"What have you done, Clarence?" they said. But Clarence was very careful to say, "It isn't me, I didn't do anything, it was Lord Lion." They were all amazed, all except Willie the Weasel, he didn't like all this excitement so he crept away. Everybody else had a party that went on for days.

ELIOT THE ELEPHANT

Eliot the elephant came from Africa, he was a very regal elephant being a court official. He was visiting a country for a holiday and was now going home, but Eliot wasn't very happy.

Clarence the cat continued his journey, he wasn't sure where he was going but he knew that Lord Lion was guarding him. All at once he saw an elephant in the distance. A voice inside him seemed to tell him to go and talk to the elephant. Clarence approached rather cautiously. After all, it was obvious that this was a very special elephant.

Eliot was saying: "Oh dear, oh dear, I don't understand it."

"Can I help you?" said Clarence.

Eliot was rather surprised to hear a voice, but said, "Yes, you see I've heard such stories in the last few days, wonderful stories about a cat and a monkey and a lion. Who is this lion?"

Clarence got excited. "Oh, I can tell you all about that". And he proceeded to tell Eliot all that had happened ending with the words:
"If you believe Lord Lion, he can do great things."

Eliot was surprised. "You mean it's as simple as that?"

"Yes", said Clarence.

"Then I will do it right now."

And that's exactly what he did and he went home very happy.

DAVEY THE DOVE

Wally the weasel sulked, he wasn't happy about what was happening, too much excitement, he preferred the old ways. Finally, he decided what he'd do, he took a group of soldiers and arrested Clarence and Eliot and had them put into prison. "That'll put an end to this nonsense."

That night Clarence lay sleeping, he wasn't too worried about being in prison, he had an idea that Lord Lion would do something, it was just a case of waiting and he was getting used to that now.

Suddenly there was a flutter of wings and there was Davey, the dove, Clarence was surprised. Eliot more so when Davey told him to follow him. "What about the soldiers?" he said, but Davey insisted and it seemed right to go along with him.

First of all, he tried the door and to his surprise it opened and they were in the corridor, but there was still the soldiers. They continued and it was just as if the soldiers were asleep, they didn't see him 'till finally they were out.

Clarence decided that the best thing to do would be to get away to another town, but first he would go and see his friends and tell them that Lord Lion had helped him escape. They were a little surprised but overjoyed to see him. After a short while Clarence began his journey.

WILLIE THE WEASEL

It was early morning when Willie, the weasel, discovered that Clarence had escaped. He was so angry that he almost made himself ill. There was only one thing to do - he would go after him.

He took a company of soldiers and set off. All the time he was thinking, "I will put an end to this dangerous nonsense if it's the last thing I do".

They had been travelling for some time when suddenly there was a flash of lightning. Willie cried out, "I can't see. My eyes! I can't see! Help!" He fell down, rolling on the ground. Suddenly there was a great roar like the sound of a lion. Willie thought he could hear a voice saying, "Stop hurting my friends." "Yes, I will, I will", he cried, "What about my eyes?" Then there was a second roar that seemed to say "Go to the town and you will be alright". So Willie limped to the next town and waited.

Clarence was hiding when he thought he heard a voice beside him saying, "Go to Willie the weasel who is in the town".

Now Clarence wasn't altogether happy about this. After all Willie had put him in prison, but he was sure the Lord Lion had something for him to do, so he went straight away.

As he entered the room he said: "Willie, I am here". And Willie cried out, "Clarence, is that you? I'm sorry for trying to hurt you and your friends. I do believe in Lord Lion now. Please forgive me."

As he said this, his eyes opened and he could see. "I can see! Oh Clarence, take me with you, I want to tell the world about Lord Lion." And that's exactly what he did.

THE FLOOD

Deep in the forest lived a rabbit called Ricky and a badger called Barry. They were very happy there until one day when it rained so hard that the water began to rise and there was danger of a flood.

"What shall we do?" asked Ricky the rabbit.

"I don't know", said Barry the badger. "We ought to move, but I'm not sure where to go."

"Yes" said Ricky, "We can't stay here or we'll drown. What we need is somebody to help us."

Just then there was a rustling in the leaves. It got louder until they saw Sammy the skunk.

"I'll help you", said Sammy, "I'll show you where to go."

Now Ricky the rabbit and Barry the badger felt a bit ashamed because they'd never really been friends with Sammy and never really wanted to know him, in fact no one did and they were worried; after all, what if he led them into a trap to pay them back for not being nice. But in the end they had to trust him.

"Come on", said Sammy. "We must be quick, I can hear the water coming!"

So Sammy led them to safety and when the floods had ended, he led them back home.

THE RACE

One day there was to be a big race with a magnificent trophy as a prize. There were three entrants: Robert the Rolls Royce; Tony the Toyota and Morris the Mini.

Now Robert the Rolls and Tony the Toyota were a bit snooty about Morris. "You won't win", they said. "You're too slow, you haven't got a chance against us!"

The race started. Robert the Rolls came to a hump-back bridge, the sign said slow down, but Robert always thought that he knew how to drive. In any case, the faster he went, the quicker he would finish the race so he went at high speed, half way across the bridge he bounced off into the river, so he couldn't finish the race.

Tony the Toyota was going along quite nicely until he came to a railway crossing. The sign said stop, but Tony thought if I stop I'll lose time. In any case, if I go as fast as I can, I'll get through before the gate closes. He started to go across, but never made it because he was hit by the train.

Morris was different. Although he was slower, he always obeyed the road signs, when it said slow, he went slow, and when it said stop, he stopped. He finished the race and won the prize.

THE MINSTREL

THE GREAT ICE CREAM MYSTERY

It was the biggest event of the century. Princess Mary was to marry Prince Colin. There was to be the biggest party ever and the big surprise was that there would be ice-cream for everyone, of whatever flavour they wanted. There was great excitement everywhere.

Just before the party was due to begin the servants came to the steward. They were trembling because they knew the steward would be angry. "What's the matter?" the steward said. "Well, sir, all the ice-cream's disappeared." "What!" shouted the steward, "All the ice-cream? What am I going to do?"

He sent the servants away and for a long time tried to think what he could do. Then, he had an idea. He slipped out of the palace and went into the forest and there he met a man dressed in green. He was a minstrel and he carried a lute. The steward didn't know much about this minstrel but the minstrel had helped him before so he said, "Look, all the ice-cream has disappeared for the party. Can you help?" "I'm not sure I can," said the minstrel, "but go back to the palace and see what happens".

The steward went back to the palace. By now, the party was in full swing, and it was nearly time for the big treat. The steward was worried, the king would be angry if there was no ice-cream. Just before it was time the steward went to the freezer and opened it. He couldn't believe his eyes. There was so much ice-cream in so many flavours, that everybody had exactly what they wanted. And that day went down in the history books as one of the best ever in that kingdom.

THE PICNIC

One day, a few years later, King Colin and Queen Moira decided to have a picnic in the forest. It was to be a very special occasion to which the whole court would come. First of all there was singing and dancing. Then a few games, then the great feast.

After this the king's son, Philip, wandered off. He went into the forest but forgot which path he had taken and soon got lost. Soon it began to get dark and he grew frightened.

The king realised that he was missing and went to look for him. He searched high and low and was beginning to get anxious, especially as he knew that the queen would be cross. Suddenly he saw the minstrel and said, "Can you help me look for my son who is lost?" The minstrel replied, "Well, I won't go with you, but I'll tell you where he is. If you take the path to the left, go through the oak tree, you'll find him there."

The king was a little surprised that the minstrel wouldn't go with him but he thought he'd better follow the instructions, and when he did he found his son and took him home safely.

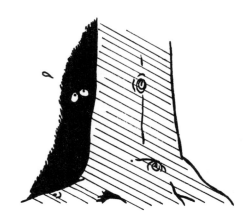

THE RESCUE

Many years later, soldiers from another land came and surrounded the castle. They captured everybody and because they didn't like the king they said that they would kill him.

In the courtyard all the soldiers lined up, and the king was put against the wall. The rest of the court were made to watch. Now just as the captain shouted, "Fire!" the minstrel rushed in and threw himself in front of the king. He was hit several times and fell down dead.

There was so much confusion that they decided they would kill the king later, so they took the whole court to a big hall and kept them there as prisoners.

Now they had left the minstrel lying on the floor. Sometime later, he began to move, slowly at first but then gradually he got to his feet, and walked towards the great hall.

Inside the hall there was silence. Suddenly the door flew open and there stood the minstrel, alive. The soldiers were terrified and ran for their lives, but the king and the queen and the court rejoiced because he had saved them. He had died and now he had come back to life.

ALFIE, THE AWKWARD APPLE

Alfie was an apple - a big, red apple - full of bounce. He looked very nice and healthy but he had one problem - he would not do what he was told, in fact he was the most awkward apple that you could ever meet. Mum and Dad were always telling him that if he didn't change something would happen - but Alfie just wouldn't listen - he knew better.

One day he went for a walk, it was a beautiful day and his Mum told him to be back by five, but of course, he wasn't - half past five, six o'clock, still no sign of Alfie; as the clock struck eight in walked Alfie and up he went to bed straight away, without even a supp of tea. On another occasion he broke a window. The more Alfie was awkward - he noticed that he wasn't looking his usual self. In fact he realised with horror that he was going rotten, or at least beginning to. There were black marks all over him.

There was great excitement - it was the great time of gathering when all the young apples would be collected up and given away to special people. This was what every apple looked forward to, but not Alfie because no one was going to pick Alfie the way he looked - he was so ugly he would be left behind until he went rotten. As he thought about this tears began to run down his face, "I wish I hadn't been so awkward" he said, sobbingly, "I'm so sorry". Then he noticed that as the tears ran down they began to remove the blackness and his old self began to appear - if I can find some water then perhaps I can be washed clean and I'll never be awkward again, and sure enough as he got into the water and promised to be good - then all the blackness disappeared and once more he was red and shiny. To tell the truth he was twice as bright and of course everyone wanted to take him. There was no chance of him being left behind.

THE HOLIDAY

There was a boy called Jimmy who had never been away on holiday. All his friends had but he hadn't. How he wished he could go away even if it was only for a week-end, even if it was just a few miles. He didn't care where it was just to go away that's all he wanted.

As the school holidays came around he felt thoroughly depressed. He asked all his friends if he could go with them but of course they said no, there was no room. Jimmy began to cry. Then one of his friends said why don't you ask Mr. G. Jimmy thought to himself, that's a good idea. Why hadn't he thought of it before, then he thought again. How do you talk to Mr. G, you can't telephone him, you can't send a letter because there's no address. There's only one thing to do I'll go and talk to the vicar.

He went round to the vicarage and asked the vicar how you talk to Mr. G. The vicar said that Mr. G was everywhere so you could just talk naturally. Jimmy thought this was strange but he decided to give it a try so he stood quite still and called out timidly. "Mr. G are you there?" At first there was no answer so he called again. Suddenly a loud voice said, "Yes, what do you want?"

"My name is Jimmy!"

"I know that" said Mr. G, "I know all about you."

"Do you?" said Jimmy surprised.

"Yes" said Mr. G. "Anyway, what is it you want?"

At this point Jimmy got a little bit nervous. Well really I want to go on holiday. I'd do anything for you, if you'd just let me go on holiday. I promise. Absolutely anything, I think."

"If I let you go on holiday" said Mr. G "Would you be my friend?"

"Is that all you want" said Jimmy, feeling relieved.

"Yes, that's all I want" said Mr. G.
"Well of course I'll be your friend."

So Jimmy went on his first holiday and he had a great time, eating rock and candy floss, riding on bumper cars, walking along the sea front and every night he thanked Mr. G, even when he got back home and had to go to school.

THE KING WHO CAME IN DISGUISE

Once in a land far away was a kingdom. The kingdom was very big, stretching for many miles. Now right in the centre of this kingdom was a small village. The people in this village were friendly towards each other but they were not so nice to those people who moved there from other villages. Somehow they weren't the same. But there was one thing the people weren't happy about; that was their king. They blamed him for everything, even the bad weather. They thought that he didn't care for them at all. Every day they complained about him and they didn't like his laws even though they were designed to help the people.

One day a stranger came to the village. He was different. He was happy, yet wise, and the things he taught were good. People began to understand what the laws meant and how they could help them and as for the strangers he accepted them and treated them just the same as the villagers. The young people of the village were drawn towards him. They loved him and spent all their time with him. But there was one who was jealous, and in a rage he set fire to one of the houses and it burnt to the ground. The people were very cross and upset for the law had been broken. The king's official came and said that unless the culprit was handed over the whole village would suffer according to the law. The king recognised the official, but the official didn't recognise the king. Now after the official went to the castle, the villages became very sad for they couldn't find out who had done it. They asked everyone, but no one would admit to it.

Now the stranger felt very sorry for the village and he decided to do something about it. He decided that he would give some money so that the house could be rebuilt, because then nobody would have to admit doing it and the village would be saved. But when he offered to do this, the one who was jealous accused him of burning down the house, and even though it wasn't true the villages turned against him. They dragged him away and they twisted all that he had said so that it said something different, and they punished him according to the law. Now the king's official came down to check that everything had been done according to the law. Now when he looked at the stranger who had been punished he was horrified because it was the king.

THE GOOD NEIGHBOUR

One day, the headmaster came into the class to announce a special scheme. All the children were encouraged to help their neighbours and at the end of the day there would be an award for the most helpful.

Now Dennis was not keen on this idea at all and he went out to play some games, but Charles did attempt to help people. Then Dennis came along and persuaded him that it was much more enjoyable to play football. They forgot about the scheme.

Lucy was quite excited about the whole idea and spent half the day trying to help people. Then Dennis and Charles came along to persuade her to join them. At first she would not listen but when they promised to buy her some sweets she went with them.

Jimmy had helped all day and was quite keen. In fact, he enjoyed it. When Dennis, Charles and Lucy came to try and persuade him to play, he would not listen to them. Then the headmaster came in and of course gave the prize to Jimmy, but afterwards he shared it with all his friends even though they had not helped.

(Parable of the Sower.)

STORIES

THEMES

SALVATION

EASTER

FAITH

THE HOLY SPIRIT

MOORLEY'S

are growing Publishers, adding several new titles to our list each year. We also undertake private publications and commissioned works.

Our range of publications
includes: **Books of Verse**
Devotional Poetry
Recitations
Drama
Bible Plays
Sketches
Nativity Plays
Passiontide Plays
Easter Plays
Demonstrations
Resource Books
Assembly Material
Songs & Musicals
Children's Addresses
Prayers & Graces
Daily Readings
Books for Speakers
Activity Books
Quizzes
Puzzles
Painting Books
Daily Readings
Church Stationery
Notice Books
Cradle Rolls
Hymn Board Numbers

Please send a S.A.E. (approx 9" x 6") for the current catalogue or consult your local Christian Bookshop who should stock or be able to order our titles.